T0198824

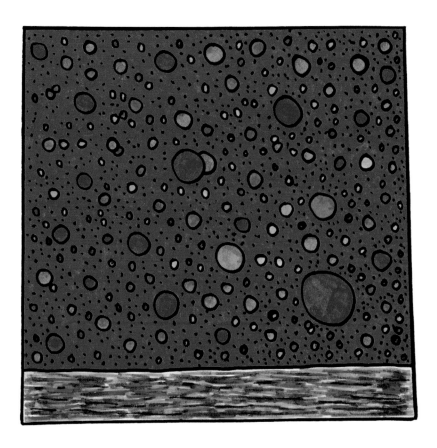

Bezebia

Just before the Harvest Season arrived, the Zetel Master sent forth a great many kings to Briskfalls.

Bezeeb

Yet to their surprise, all of the realm was corrupted.

Side View Of Bezeb Interior

So the Zetel Master became very angry.

Zetel Warped

Sokhen and Sokhit were captured and held in bondage inside the Emanation Vessel.

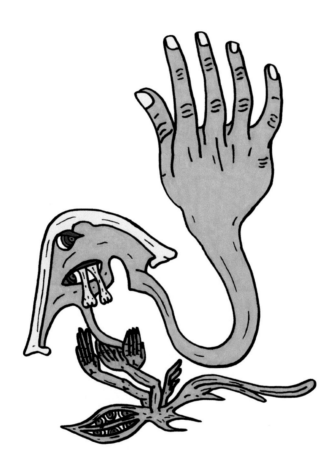

Dispompacy

Until their purity cleansed Briskfalls' entirety.

Zetel Master

Purified, the Neffrey filled the infinite realmscape from top to bottom with an overinfinite abundance of zetel.

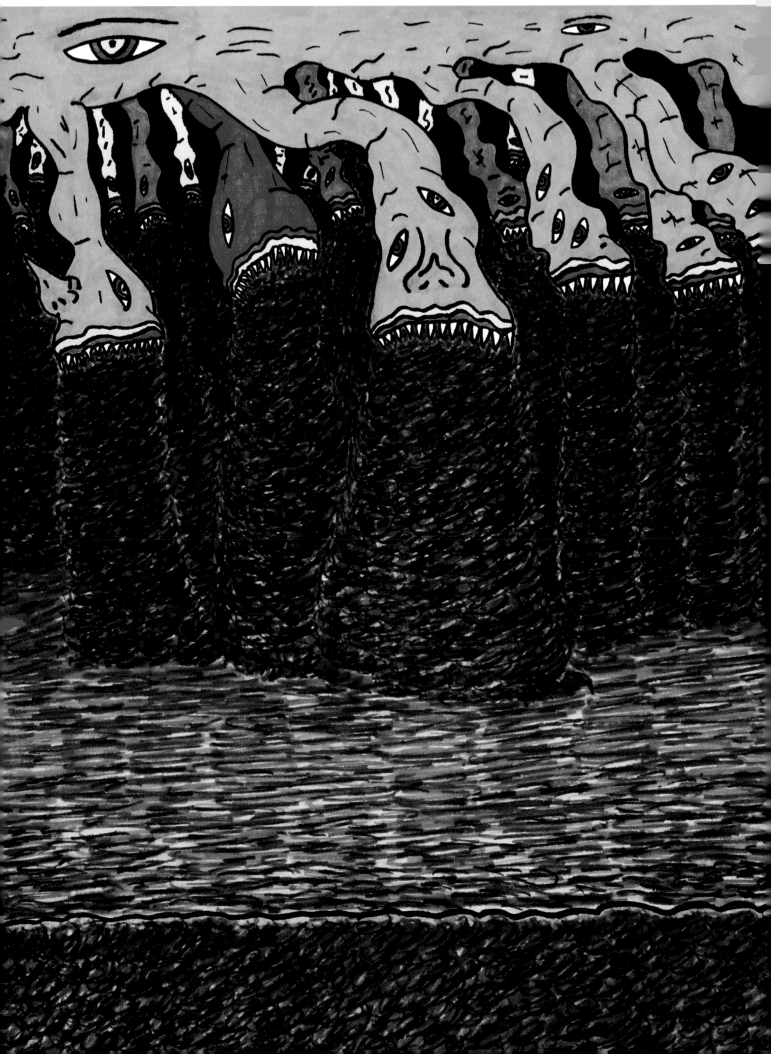

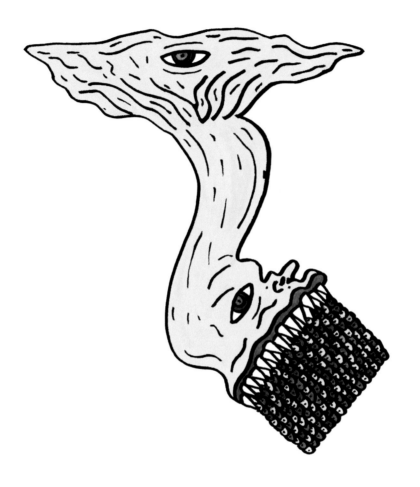

Neffrey Spawning Zetel

And the Zetel Master's servants gathered
Her Majesty's tribute.

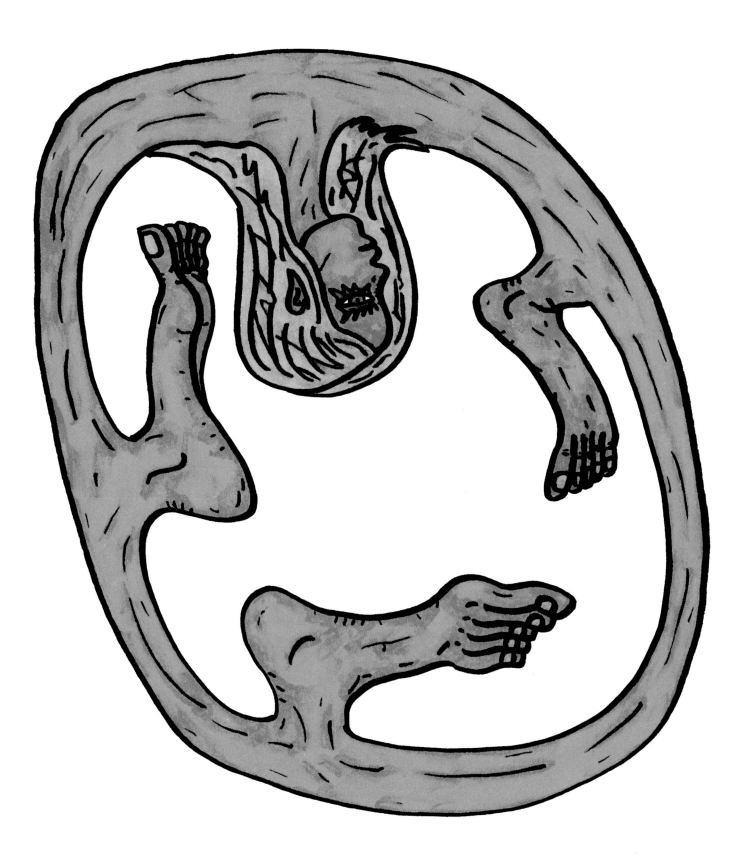

Zetel Reformation

Order this book online at www.trafford.com
or email orders@trafford.com

Most Trafford titles are also available at major online book retailers.

 www.trafford.com

North America & international
toll-free: 844 688 6899 (USA & Canada)
fax: 812 355 4082

Our mission is to efficiently provide the world's finest, most
comprehensive book publishing service, enabling every author to
experience success. To find out how to publish your book, your way,
and have it available worldwide, visit us online at www.trafford.com

Because of the dynamic nature of the Internet, any web addresses or
links contained in this book may have changed since publication and
may no longer be valid. The views expressed in this work are solely those
of the author and do not necessarily reflect the views of the publisher,
and the publisher hereby disclaims any responsibility for them.

Any people depicted in stock imagery provided by Getty Images are models,
and such images are being used for illustrative purposes only.
Certain stock imagery © Getty Images.

ISBN: 978-1-4251-6830-8 (e)

Print information available on the last page.

Trafford rev. 03/05/2021

Printed in the United States
by Baker & Taylor Publisher Services